American History Poems

by Bobbi Katz

SCHOLASTIC
PROFESSIONAL BOOKS

NEW YORK • TORONTO • LONDON • AUCKLAND • SYDNEY

For Liza Charlesworth

Acknowledgments

My thanks to the educators who generously gave me suggestions for making activities more useful for classroom teachers: Jacqui Anderson, a math specialist; Beth Glazeroff, who teaches both children and teachers; Carol Shank, a classroom teacher; and Dr. Regina White, a past president of the New York State Social Studies Supervisory Association, who currently serves on the New York State Council for the Social Studies. I also wish to give a big cheer to Maria Sweeney and her fourth grade class at the Hawes School in Ridgewood, New Jersey. They reinforce my belief that when a good teacher respects and challenges children, they will stretch beyond expected boundaries to do amazing work and grasp complex issues.

Cover design by Vincent Ceci and Jaime Lucero
Cover art by Alexandra Wallner
Interior design by Solutions by Design, Inc.
Interior art by Mona Mark

ISBN 0-590-49973-4

Table of Contents

Introduction

I was delighted when my editor asked if I'd like to create poems and activities based on the social studies curriculum. Remembering what fun I'd had many years ago compiling two books on American folklore, it didn't take me long to say, "you bet!" While I had recently written a biography of Nelson Mandela and had edited books on Martin Luther King, Jr., and John F. Kennedy, my recreational reading is usually about nature and science. This challenging project would give me a chance to take an overdue refresher course in one of my favorite subjects as well provide an opportunity to help educators spark and nourish a lively interest in our country's history. What's more, I would be able to do both of these things through poetry! It's the kind of writing closest to my heart and a way of reaching kids that I believe really works.

Armed with a list of topics from my editor, I started reading a generalized history of the United States to get the big picture, and my excitement grew. What a panorama was spread before me. As I began subject-specific research, I found myself drawn to letters, journals, and personal accounts. I read biographies and studied old photographs and paintings. How could I make kids feel the excitement I was feeling? Which tidbits from the feast of facts I was devouring would be most useful to classroom teachers?

Early on I decided to write all the poems in the first person. That seemed the best way to bring the past closer to the lives of present-day children. I not only tried to imagine what it would have felt like to have been Thomas Jefferson as he thought about writing the Declaration of Independence or George Washington as he rode to the very first inauguration of an elected head of state, but I also tried to climb into the personalities of the countless anonymous people—both children and adults—who have been part of America's story. So many voices beckoned to be given words! It was difficult to choose between them. I knew that whomever I spoke for had to be a specific individual—someone who became real for me—or the result would be a collection of paper dolls.

I needed to really know that ten-year-old boy traveling across the Oregon Trail month after month in what had become his only home—

a Conestoga wagon. The details of his life are different, but how different could *he* have been from my own children, who got antsy after a couple of hours in a comfortable car? And the pioneer woman who was miles from a neighbor and months from even a letter—was she so very different from me and my friends, who depend on each other for advice, sympathy, company, and laughter? How might a conversation between neighboring children reflect the conflicting political positions of their parents? How might the great venture of building railroads across the country have felt to a Chinese laborer? I hope that you and the students you teach will be engaged by the voices of these individuals. They speak through me in the context of their personal experiences of their times. Whether using actual or fictional characters, I have tried to make each topic come to life through voices that ring with the authenticity of real people.

Some poems are light and funny. Some are short encapsulations of an experience. And some are long narratives that tell a story. A suffragette sings a song to the tune of "The Battle Hymn of the Republic" as she marches for voting rights. Meriwether Lewis makes a list as he leaves to meet William Clark for their fantastic expedition to the Pacific. Old Abe—not the venerable President (who, of course, has his own poem) but the venerable regimental mascot of the 8th Wisconsin—will give you a bird's-eye view of the Civil War. Old Abe was an eagle, carried into battle tethered on a perch alongside of the regimental colors.

While some poems are more difficult than others, educators tell me that those relating to holidays such as Thanksgiving and "the birthdays" (Washington, Lincoln, Martin Luther King, Jr.) are within the grasp of the younger student but still meaty enough to satisfy the older one.

When it came to background information and activities, I asked classroom teachers what *they* wanted and needed, what useful tools I could give them. They generously responded with intelligence and creativity—and variety, assuring me that teachers use activities as "sparks," adapting them for their students.

While there are map and math skills based on the topics, I've also tried to relate the past to the present by drawing parallels to current events. Teachers encouraged me to provide activities that will raise consciousness about values. Not every activity or poem will be appropriate for your class; nevertheless, I hope you'll find many that will serve as launching pads for various topics.

One big surprise was that almost all of the poems rhyme, even the more serious ones. (And I had been *so* careful to make sure that Scholastic wouldn't require me to write in rhyme all of the time!) It's as if the momentum of the growing nation carried me along on its rhythms. I hope this book will make history hum with life and energy for you and your students, as researching and writing it did for me. I offer these poems to you as springboards of rhyme and rhythm with which to explore our American heritage.

The First Americans

When ice blankets you call glaciers,
were moving, slowly moving,
we found an open passage
between their frozen walls.
And we took that rich green passage,
in small bands we took that passage,
following the bison,
    following the game.
        Finding as we followed,
          nuts and berries,
            elk and deer.

Mother Earth and Father Sun,
hear the voices of your children,
thankful voices of your children,
for the gifts you made appear!

Ours were the first voices.
The first voices were The People.
Now we whisper
when the winds blow.
Remember we were here.

Over the Top of the World

How and when did the first Americans begin their trek over the top of the world? During the Ice Age, the present-day Bering Strait became a bridge of dry land that scholars call Beringia. Using carbon dating, scientists have determined that at least 30,000 years ago, small groups of Asian hunters looking for food began entering the hills of what is now Alaska.

As the "People of the Dawn" spread throughout the Americas, they developed various life styles and customs in response to the different environments they encountered. Some remained hunters; others became farmers. They spoke different languages. They were the ancestors of the Pueblo, the Algonquin, the Zuni, the Kwakiutl, the Inuit, and the Incas, among other groups. One thing all Native Americans shared was a reverence for the forces of nature.

VOCABULARY

glacier: thick sheet of ice

bison: large animal that has a big shaggy head with short horns and a humped back; buffalo

Discussion Question Read this expression of Native American philosophy to your students: "The earth does not belong to The People. The People belong to the earth." Ask them to discuss what message this has for Americans today.

Writing Prompt Over two million Native Americans are currently living in the United States. Have students write a four-line poem that begins: *Remember we are here.*

Extension Activity Have students work in groups to prepare reports on various groups of Native Americans to present to the class. Encourage them to include maps, pictures artifacts, and tapes of music relating to these different cultures.

A Pilgrim Boy

William Hopkins: Plymouth, England, September 5, 1620

We were cruelly scorned in England,
when we wished to have our say
of just how we should worship God
and keep His Sabbath day.
Many families fled to Holland,
a fair—but worldly—nation.
Then our leaders got a patent
to establish a plantation—
a plantation in the New World
where we will fish and farm—
where we will follow our own ways
not fearing jail or harm.
Now we're anchored in the harbor.
On the morning tide, we sail.
It will be a great adventure.
With God's grace we cannot fail!

AMERICAN HISTORY POEMS
Scholastic Professional Books, 1998

A Pilgrim Boy

The Pilgrims

The Pilgrims were actually made up of two groups of people who had very different reasons for wanting to start a colony in America. Half of them, called Separatists, were seeking religious freedom. The other half, called Strangers, wanted to own land and make money.

In 1608 the Separatists had left England for Holland where their religious views were tolerated. But many missed the English way of life, and so they decided to move to America. There they would still be English subjects but be free to worship as they wished.

The Separatists did not have enough money for a ship or supplies and were not a large enough group to start a colony. They found some London merchants to finance their trip. In return, the Separatists agreed to clear land, build homes, and work for the merchants for seven years. The merchants found other planters to join the Separatists—people the Separatists called Strangers. They planned to settle in Virginia, an area which was much larger and extended further north than the present-day state of Virginia.

The *Mayflower's* trip across the Atlantic was a long and difficult one. Severe storms battered the ship. Many people became ill, and all were confined below deck for long periods. The storms blew the ship off course. When land was finally sighted by those on board, it was not Virginia they saw, but Cape Cod in New England.

VOCABULARY

scorn: to treat as low or bad

Sabbath: the day of the week that is used for worship

plantation: a colony or new settlement

patent: a written grant giving a person or company certain rights; patents are issued by the government

Discussion Question Leaving England for a new life was an exciting but terrifying prospect for the Pilgrims. Encourage students to take a stand: If they had been Pilgrims, would they have gone or stayed behind? As they discuss their decisions, encourage them to give specific reasons for their choices.

Writing Prompt While some family groups sailed together on the Mayflower, others split up with one or more members remaining behind in England or the Netherlands. Ask students to write one or two diary entries from the point of view of either a mother who had left a child behind or a child whose parents were sailing alone.

Extension Activity The Pilgrims, their indentured servants, and their crew were "packed like herrings" on the *Mayflower*. Families had to pack their things in small chests. Bring a standard-size moving carton to class. Ask students to imagine they are starting a new life in a strange place. Tell them they can only bring what will fit inside the carton. After they measure the carton, have them determine if their items will fit inside. They should also explain the choices they have made.

My Favorite Time

Elizabeth Brandon: Windsor, Connecticut, November, 1752

In the evenings after supper,
when all of our chores are done,
our family gathers near the hearth
for some restful, quiet fun.
I helped make the tallow candles.
Now their warm and gentle glow
casts soft light upon my sampler
as I settle down to sew.
In the center winding roses
rise around our cottage door.
Some day they may look just that way,
when they grow a little more.
Mother wove the sturdy homespun;
Father made the willow frame.
And now carefully I'll cross-stitch
the year…
and then…
my name.

My Favorite Time
Colonial Life

Try to imagine how difficult colonial life was. Many of the first colonists had been trades people or crafts workers in England. In the colonies, they learned to be farmers—to clear land, to care for animals, to grow food. They had to be carpenters and seamstresses. Although many colonists had servants, there was no shortage of chores to be done. Children were expected to do their share from an early age.

In Connecticut, where Elizabeth Brandon lived, every town of more than fifty families was required to hire a teacher and set up a school. Children in outlying areas were taught the basics by their parents. Either way, schooling was tucked in between feeding the chickens, milking the cows, and just helping out.

VOCABULARY

tallow: fat from cattle and sheep that is used to make candles

sampler: a cloth embroidered with designs in different stitches

homespun: a cloth that is woven by hand at home

Discussion Question Sewing her sampler and spending quiet time with her family at the end of the day was Elizabeth's idea of fun. Ask kids to talk about what makes some work fun and what's good or bad about "quiet times."

Writing Prompt By the time Elizabeth made her sampler, spinning wheels—rare in the 17th century home—were common. The poorly balanced wooden ax with a strip of iron along the edge had been replaced by the light-weight American ax. Wooden plows were in use. By 1700 more and more people were using table forks, which meant knives could be used for cutting food, rather than for spearing it. "What's next?" asked some in outrage. "If we were meant to use forks, why were we given fingers?" What would these folks say about airplanes? computers? space exploration? other modern conveniences? Have students write a skit using their responses.

Extension Activity New Englanders made most of the everyday items they needed. Have students choose and research a topic, such as glass blowing or candle making, and create an illustrated flow chart showing each of the steps involved in making the item.

A Tea Merchant's Daughter

Abagail Shelton: Boston, 1773

My father's in a fury.
    And so are all his friends.
England treats us like we're chattel
    to use for its own ends.
England thinks that we Colonials
    have no right to make choices.
They disregard our envoys.
    English ears can't hear our voices.

Now bankruptcy is facing
    their most precious company.
England wants to save it.
    At what cost?
    Our liberty!
They've cut tea taxes to three pence.
    But what's wrong?
    A monopoly!
Just *their* chosen few are allowed to sell
    British East Indian tea.

Tea merchants like my father
    can buy fine tea from the Dutch.
We don't need tea from England.
    Thank you very much!

A party's planned in Boston.
    Who's coming?
They'll be many.
    Will there be cups of British tea?
Tea, yes!
    But cups.... Not any.

AMERICAN HISTORY POEMS
Scholastic Professional Books, 1998

A Tea Merchant's Daughter

No Milk, No Sugar: The Boston Tea Party

Ships belonging to the British East India Company transported tea to England. When the tea was exported to America, Great Britain added high taxes. "Taxation without representation" was already a rallying cry, but the taxes on tea were so outrageous that the colonists openly bought smuggled tea from the Dutch East India Company. Finally, with the British East India Company facing bankruptcy and London warehouses packed with tea, the British government decided to lower the tax to three pence a pound. England expected the Americans to be thankful, but many were outraged. Only a few hand-picked British agents were allowed to sell the tea and collect the tax; American tea merchants could have been put out of business.

On December 16, 1773, bands of colonists disguised as Indians boarded three English ships that were packed with chests of loose tea. They dumped the tea into Boston Harbor. England responded by closing the port, effectively cutting off the colonists from trade and travel.

VOCABULARY

chattel: an item of personal property, such as a chair or a car

envoy: messenger

bankruptcy: when a person or business cannot pay its debts

pence: in Britain, more than one penny

monopoly: the sole control of a product or service by a person or company

merchant: a person whose business is buying and selling things

Discussion Question The men who threw the tea overboard were breaking the law. Ask students why we consider them heroes rather than criminals. Is it ever right to break the law? Have students explain their answers.

Writing Prompt Ask students to imagine they are American tea merchants at risk of losing their businesses. Have them write letters to the British government protesting "taxation without representation."

Extension Activity Have students create a skit re-enacting the Boston Tea Party. Some students should be colonists, while others take the role of British agents.

A Conversation on the Edge of War

Amos Davis and Esther Gomez: Newport, September, 1774

I am a loyal British child,
a subject of the King.
And I would not be otherwise.
No. Not for anything.

> *You're a spineless little Tory.*
> *You're as brainless as a flea—*
> *too gutless to want freedom*
> *in a land with liberty!*

You're a traitor to your country
without proper loyalties.
You speak of "independence."
We are British colonies.

> *Tax us! Tax us! Please, dear King.*
> *Deny us every right.*
> *But do not be surprised, dear King,*
> *if we're prepared...*
> > *to fight!*

AMERICAN HISTORY POEMS
Scholastic Professional Books, 1998

Two Points of View

Many Americans, including George Washington, hoped for a reasonable accommodation with Great Britain on taxation. When British repression escalated after the Boston Tea Party, hopes for a peaceful solution faded. Washington dreaded the bloodshed of war. As the Revolutionary War began with incidents, skirmishes, and full-fledged battles, the loyalties of many colonials were torn by such connections. Firebrands such as Patrick Henry and Samuel Adams could not stir them to take up arms against "Mother England." Some colonists actively helped the British. There were disagreements between neighbors and even within families.

You may wonder about Esther Gomez. Sephardic Jews, whose ancestors came from Spain, began arriving in the colonies in the 17th century. They were staunch supporters of independence. When it appeared that New York would become a British stronghold, many Jews, including the Gomezes, left New York and moved to the colony of Rhode Island. (Emma Lazarus, who wrote the poem for the Statue of Liberty, was a descendant of the Gomez family.)

VOCABULARY

Tory: in the Revolutionary War, a person who was loyal to Great Britain; also called a Loyalist

traitor: a person who betrays his or her country

Discussion Question Encourage the class to discuss why the issue of loyalty is often the subject of passionate debate among people who have different views. Ask students how family members can disagree over an issue but still remain loyal to each other.

Writing Prompt Have students pretend that they are Esther Gomez. Then ask them to write letters to Amos Davis explaining the need for independence.

Extension Activity Remind the class that large numbers of colonists remained loyal to Great Britain during the Revolutionary War. Have students research the Loyalists in America. Then invite them to create a pamphlet that outlines the Loyalists' argument for supporting Great Britain.

The Challenge

Thomas Jefferson: Philadelphia, June 11, 1776

After being forced to quarter
    British troops who burn and kill,
After laws were made mere mockeries
    the King could change at will,
After losing every basic right,
    after death and desolation,
it's time that we must choose to be
    a free and sovereign nation.
After Lexington and Concord,
    after Crown Point and Breed Hill,
the people of America
    have had more than their fill!

Now I have the solemn duty
    to draft a Declaration
making thirteen colonies
    an independent nation.
My head must guide my heart and hand,
    as my hand guides this pen,
to write words worthy of a land
    with justice for all men.

AMERICAN HISTORY POEMS
Scholastic Professional Books, 1998

The Declaration of Independence:

"An Expression of the American Mind"

George Washington was already leading colonial troops into battle when the Continental Congress appointed a committee to draft a declaration supporting its resolution to sever ties with Great Britain. Benjamin Franklin, John Adams, Robert Livingston, and Roger Sherman, as well as Thomas Jefferson, were all on the committee. But it was Jefferson who wrote the first draft. Many years later, Jefferson insisted that all he tried to do was to provide "an expression of the American mind."

Over 90 other "declarations of independence" had been issued by various towns, colonies, and artisan groups, so Jefferson did not question the urgency of his task. His well-reasoned, eloquent text was presented to Congress with only a few minor revisions. The Declaration was then unanimously passed by Congress on July 4, 1776, and signed by John Hancock on its behalf. On August 11, 1776, all 56 members of the Continental Congress signed the Declaration, which had been exquisitely embossed on parchment. It is this version that is familiar to us and has become a treasured link with our heroic past.

VOCABULARY

quarter: to provide lodging for soldiers

mockery: a person or thing that is made fun of

desolation: a condition of being destroyed or ruined

sovereign: independent of all others

Lexington and Concord; Crown Point and Breed Hill: the location of battles fought during the revolutionary war

Discussion Question Sometimes the Declaration uses the word *people* and sometimes *men*. The word *women* never appears. New Jersey decided it gave women the right to vote, and women did vote in that state until the Constitution took effect in 1791. Ask students if they think "the founding fathers" purposely excluded "the founding mothers?" Did the word *men* imply both men and women? all humans?

Writing Prompt It's 1776! Each of your students is a newspaper reporter whose job it is to describe the debates over the Declaration of Independence. Have each student research the position of one of the colonies and present his or her findings in a newspaper article.

Extension Activity Ask students to find a tape or book of songs about the Revolutionary War. Have them work in groups to prepare a presentation to the class. Each presentation might include an explanation of the songs as well as singing some of the songs.

Inauguration Day Thoughts

George Washington: New York, April 30, 1789

What a heavy obligation—
I must not betray the trust
of this fledgling little nation.
I must start out right. I must.
The War gave us a common cause.
Now loud voices of dissent
grow sharper than a jaguar's claws—
raised to strike in discontent.

I must show by words and actions
how free men resolve their fights.
I must balance all the factions—
calm the zealots for states' rights.
I must set the first example
of what a President should be,
as I walk
     on untrodden ground
with
     no path
        in place
     for
me.

Inauguration Day Thoughts

"I Walk on Untrodden Ground":

The First President

Although George Washington had little formal education, the young man impressed his well-to-do Virginia neighbors with his intelligence and geniality. As a general, Washington had shown that a highly trained army could be defeated by courage and ingenuity. Now, as president, could he prove to the world that people were capable of governing themselves? That was a very new and very radical idea!

When Washington was elected the first president of the United States in 1789, he accepted with mixed feelings. He longed to devote his tremendous energies to his farm: to acquiring lands in the wilderness, to promoting the building of canals, to breeding his horses, and to designing gardens at his home in Mount Vernon. Yet who else but George Washington could keep the nation from anarchy and transform the Constitution into a working government?

VOCABULARY

dissent: a strong difference of opinion

faction: group of people working for a particular cause

zealot: a person with a strong devotion to a particular idea or cause

untrodden: something that has never been walked on before

Discussion Question The poem surmises what Washington might have been thinking as he traveled to his inauguration. In a letter, he wrote, "I walk on untrodden ground." Encourage students to discuss why being the first president was so important. Ask: What thoughts might candidates have today as they ride to their inauguration in Washington, D.C.?

Writing Prompt Ask students to notice the last few lines of the poem. Encourage them to discuss why the poet wrote the words the way she did. How does the placement of the words reflect the meaning of the words? Encourage kids to write a few lines of free verse and experiment with breaking lines to emphasize meaning.

Extension Activity This poem contains some strong imagery: the jaguar's claw and the untrodden path, for example. Suggest that students use these images to create political cartoons related to Washington's inauguration. Be sure to share some sample cartoons with them first.

My White House Education

Sharon Gilligan: The White House January, 1803

The Louisiana Purchase
    took most folks by surprise,
but I saw it in the making
    right before these very eyes.
All those dinners keep us busy,
    but I love my job! It's true.
While serving soup called *consomme*,
    I find out what is new:
What's worrying the President?
What does Congress want to do?

Mr. James Monroe ate fish *filet*,
    before sailing off to France
to give Minister Livingston's mission
    more strength—a better chance.
What was it?
    To buy New Orleans,
    which slick Spain in a secret deal
had ceded back to foxy France.
    And then…sought to conceal.

AMERICAN HISTORY POEMS
Scholastic Professional Books, 1998

Just as I served the *tarte des pommes*,
    the President made mention
that he did not trust Napoleon.
    What was that one's sly intention?
Extending the French Empire
    to the West of our young nation!
We'd be forced to turn to Britain.
    What a vexing situation!

"The Constitution fails to say
    if our country has the right
to buy new territories,
    but I'd rather buy than fight!"

"Dear friend," said Mr. James Monroe,
    as I filled his cup with tea,
"We can't afford to risk a war.
    On that point, we both agree!"

I never had a chance to learn
    how to read or how to write.
But I get an education
    at the White House every night!

My White House Education
The Louisiana Purchase

Soon after becoming president, Thomas Jefferson learned that Spain had returned the Louisiana Territory to France. Spain had been given this vast territory in 1763, at the end of the French and Indian War. Since then the United States had been allowed to navigate the Mississippi River and to export cargo from New Orleans. This port city was vital to American farmers and fur trappers. But with France now controlling this region, would New Orleans and the Mississippi be closed to Americans? Napoleon, France's emperor, had conquered most of Europe and was trying to expand France's holdings in the Caribbean. Would the United States be next? Torn by fears of overstepping the Constitution, Jefferson privately instructed his Minister to France to buy not only the east bank of the Mississippi, which Congress had approved, but also the Floridas and New Orleans as well. He sent his friend James Monroe to France to clinch the deal. But by the time Monroe arrived, Napoleon had already made an astounding counter offer: the whole of the Louisiana Territory, including New Orleans, for $15 million!

VOCABULARY

consomme: French word for broth

filet: French word meaning a slice of meat or fish without bones

conceal: to hide

tarte des pommes: French words for apple pie

Napoleon: emperor of France from 1804 to 1815

vexing: troubling

Discussion Question Narrative poems tell a story. Have students discuss what this poem says about the background of the Louisiana Purchase. Ask: How does it reflect Jefferson's personal style and philosophy? (Hint: He had a French chef.)

Writing Prompt Have students locate the area of the Louisiana Purchase on a map. Then ask them to write a paragraph explaining why the region was so important to American farmers and fur trappers.

Extension Activity The United States paid about 4¢ an acre for the Louisiana Purchase. Have students research the cost of an acre of land in the area where you live. Have them determine how many acres of land they could purchase for $15 million dollars.

What I Must Take

Meriwether Lewis: Pittsburgh, Pennsylvania, August 31, 1803

All I know
of
frontier skills
astronomy
surveying
maps
geography
cooking
math
geology
animals
Indians
botany
herbal cures…
curiosity
and a
double dose of…
bravery!

What I Must Take

The Lewis and Clark Expedition:

Courage Unlimited

From the earliest days of independence, Thomas Jefferson had tried to encourage exploration of the West. He was certain there was a waterway to the Pacific Ocean. The Louisiana Purchase (1803) gave him the opportunity to send his energetic secretary, Captain Meriwether Lewis, on an expedition of this uncharted land. In addition to having Lewis draw accurate maps of the region, the President told him to take notes on everything he saw—landforms, animals, plants, Indians, and more.

Lewis was certainly well-qualified. Not only was he schooled in botany, he also was an expert hunter, woodsman, and soldier. And like Jefferson, he had wide-ranging interests and a passion to increase both his own knowledge and that of future generations.

As he planned the expedition, Lewis quickly realized that he needed another officer to come along. He chose William Clark, under whom he had served in the army. On a rainy day in May 1804, the two men left St. Louis, Missouri, with tools, food, and clothing. Their crew brought along enthusiasm, loyalty, and the courage to face the unknown.

VOCABULARY

astronomy: the study of the sun, stars, planets, and other heavenly bodies

surveying: measuring land to find out its boundaries, shape, or size

geology: the study of the history of the earth

botany: the study of plants

Discussion Question William Clark was a perfect choice for a co-captain. His skills complemented those of Lewis. For example, he was a better sailor and mapmaker. Ask students to discuss what they would look for in a co-captain if they were going on an important, dangerous mission.

Writing Prompt Ask kids to imagine the many items Lewis and Clark needed to assemble for their expedition! They needed to bring rifles, tools, food, trading beads, compasses, medicines and much more. Encourage students to research other items they might have taken. Then have them write a list poem. Remind them that the poem doesn't need to rhyme.

Extension Activity Because cameras had not yet been invented in 1803, Lewis and Clark had to rely on their own drawings and descriptions to explain the unknown animals they encountered. Provide your students with pictures of animals Lewis and Clark could have seen, such as grizzly bears, prairie dogs, and big-horned sheep. Have them write descriptions of the animals. They should exchange their descriptions with classmates to see if they can guess the animal being described.

A Seaman's Shanty

Skippy McGee: aboard the *Sea Lion*, 1812

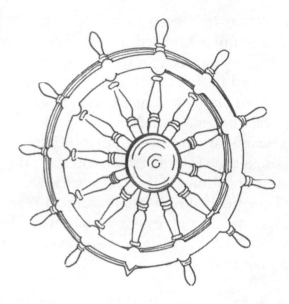

A sailor's life! A sailor's life!
    Now that's the life for me.
I signed aboard a merchant ship
    to sail across the sea.
We left from Savannah—
    stars and stripes strung high.
Climbing up the rigging,
    A happy man was I.

A British ship! A battle ship
    with cannon and the Union Jack!
Our captain let the press crew board,
    when facing an attack.
They claimed I was an Englishman,
    and took four mates and me,
although we're all Americans
    as anyone can see.

A sailor's life? A sailor's life?
    This is no life for me.
A tar upon a British ship,
    I am no longer free.
And I can only curse the day,
    I chose to go to sea.
And I can only curse the day,
    I chose to go to sea.

A Seaman's Shanty
The War of 1812

When James Madison became president in 1809, England and France were at war with each other in Europe. At first American shipping profited from the fighting. But when the French navy was destroyed by the British at the Battle of Trafalgar in 1806, Napoleon tried a new tactic—blocking British trade with Europe. Britain responded by blockading ports under French control and requiring American vessels bound for Europe to be searched in Britain and to pay a tax. Not surprisingly, these measures hurt American shipping. While some daring merchant ships ran the blockade, most limited their trade to Britain.

British sea captains were required to have a certain number of seamen. However, conditions were often so terrible on British ships that captains turned to debtors' prisons for their crew. Seamen frequently jumped ship in American ports, and many found work on American vessels. Well-armed British ships, always in need of seamen, stopped unarmed American vessels to search for deserters, whom they would *impress* back into British service. More often than not, press crews, as they were called, "accidentally" took American seamen like Skippy McGee. Although the United States protested, the practice continued. Finally, President Madison, pushed by a small group of War Hawks, asked Congress to declare war. On June 18, 1812, his request was granted by a slim majority.

VOCABULARY

rigging: all the lines of a boat or ship

Union Jack: the flag of Great Britain

press crew: British officers who came aboard American merchant ships looking for British deserters

tar: a British sailor

Discussion Question A shanty is a rhythmic work song sung by sailors as they hoisted sails or lifted an anchor. Have each of three groups of kids take turns reading a stanza of the poem, emphasizing its rhythms. Is "shanty" a good title for this poem?

Writing Prompt "The Star-Spangled Banner" was written by a Washington lawyer named Francis Scott Key during the War of 1812. Key had gone aboard a British warship in Baltimore to win the release of an American being held prisoner. All night long Key watched anxiously as British warships battered Fort McHenry. In the morning, when he saw "the flag was still waving," he expressed his relief and joy in a poem. Key's words were set to music and later became our national anthem. Encourage students to write about why they think "The Star-Spangled Banner" was chosen to be our national anthem.

Extension Activity Have students create a bulletin-board display showing the War of 1812. Tell students to include a map as well as a time line showing the important battles fought in the war.

Wondering

Ezra Smathers: Oregon Territory, August, 1843

All I asked was, "Pa, you reckon
     that we're half way there?"
Pa snarled back like a wild she-bear,
"You ask that question ten times a day!"
(I don't. No, I don't. But I didn't dare say.)

When we left Independence four months ago,
I didn't know time could ever run so slow.
At first it was fun riding up here all day,
seeing new places along the way—
    deserts and prairies—
             a wild river flood
with our wheels cutting ruts through the dust and the mud—
seeing strange critters I've never seen before—
    moose and rattlers—
      buffalo by the score.

Past Laramie,
South Pass,
then Fort Hall—
through woods so full of giant trees
no sky poked through at all.

When we stop for the night, it's
    "Fetch water."
      "Find wood."
  "Rock the baby."
      "Stir the pot."
"Listen up."
      "Be good."

And always, always, always, it's
"Don't stray away!"
And never, never, never is it
"Run off and play!"
Ma says in Vancouver,
there'll be playing time to spare.
I just wonder what Pa reckons.
 Are we half-way there?

Wondering
Along the Oregon Trail

The 1840s saw the first surge of settlers heading out along the Oregon Trail. In 1843 over a thousand families in covered wagons went west toward the Oregon Territory, which later became the states of Washington, Oregon, Idaho, and Montana.

When Easterners heard stories about the rich soil, good harbors, and fish-filled rivers of the West, they hurried to pack up their belongings and hit the road. Usually groups of 50 to 100 families gathered together in Missouri, where they began their long journey west along the Oregon Trail. Covered wagons laden with everything from clothes and furniture to farm animals and pets dotted the route to Oregon. Unhappily, hardship was not uncommon. These hearty pioneers experienced extreme cold, hunger, and thirst as well as prairie fires and buffalo stampedes.

VOCABULARY

Independence: city located in western Missouri

prairie: a gently rolling plain covered with tall, thick grass

Laramie: fort in Wyoming, located on the Oregon Trail

South Pass: pass in the Wind River Range in Wyoming

Fort Hall: former fort along the Oregon Trail in southeastern Idaho

Vancouver: a fort located at the end of the Oregon Trail

Discussion Question Nearly 500,000 people traveled west on the Oregon Trail in search of rich farmland during the 1840s and 1850s. Today each year thousands of families move from one part of the country to another. Have students discuss why families today might decide to move.

Writing Prompt Has anyone ever taken a trip and *not* wondered, "Are we halfway there?" It took six months to travel the 2,000 miles of the Oregon Trail! Ask students to think about the longest trip they have ever taken. Have them imagine how it must have felt to be traveling for six months cooped up in a covered wagon (with no heat or air-conditioning!). Add to that the problems of finding water, diseases such as cholera, and the danger of being attacked. Have students write a diary entry telling what one day might have been like along the Oregon Trail.

Extension Activity Have students find out more about the covered wagons that traveled west. Then encourage them to draw or paint a picture showing scenes of wagon trains on the Oregon Trail. Encourage them to discuss why these covered wagons were nicknamed "prairie schooners."

☆ **28** ☆

Career Plans

Abner O'Leary: St. Joseph, Missouri, April, 1860

What am I gonna be?
Come on.
Take a guess!
I'm gonna be a rider
for the Pony Express.
I'll hop on a horse
right here in St. Joe.
Like a streak of lightening,
off I'll go!
Riding, riding, riding…
fast as can be.
In ten miles
the next guy will take off like me!
Black horse…
pinto…
chestnut mare…
Riding, riding, riding
with no time to spare!
Whizzing past the stagecoach…
past the buffalo…
Folks no sooner see us coming,
then they'll see us go!
Palomino pony…
dapple gray…
Giddy-up!
Giddy-up!
Yippee-ki-ay!
I'll get mail to Sacramento
in ten days or less,
when I get to be a rider
for the Pony Express!

Career Plans

Clear the Way for the Pony Express!

A letter from home was enough to make a gold prospector put down his pan or a lumberjack drop his ax. The government postal service couldn't keep up with the growth of the West, so a bevy of private express companies, such as Wells Fargo, took on the job. In towns there were express offices at stores or banks. Mule trains brought supplies and mail to workers in remote camps. But nothing made a more vivid impression than the Pony Express! For five dollars a letter, Pony Express riders raced across the 2,000 miles of prairies and mountains from St. Joseph, Missouri, to Sacramento, California, thrilling whoever saw them speed by.

Just as the poem says, it was a relay. A letter was passed on to a new rider and horse every ten miles. A full trip took just ten days.

VOCABULARY

pinto: a horse or pony that has spots or patches of two or more colors

Sacramento: capital of California

palomino: a light tan horse having a cream-colored or white mane and tail

Discussion Question Abner O'Leary never got a chance to be a rider for the Pony Express. The company went out of business in just 18 months, when coast-to-coast telegraph service made it obsolete. Encourage students to discuss how recent technology has changed the way people communicate. What jobs or skills are no longer needed?

Writing Prompt Have students imagine that they are pioneers awaiting the arrival of the Pony Express. Tell them to write a journal entry describing their feelings when they first see a Pony Express rider appear on the horizon.

Extension Activity Invite students to make up math problems related to the Pony Express. For example, have them figure out how many Pony Express riders rode each day and the total number of miles they covered per day. What was the per-mile cost of a Pony Express letter? Have them write their problems on one side of an index card and exchange them with classmates. Classmates can write their answers on the other side.

Freedom!

Harriet Tubman: Auburn, New York, December, 1860

I knew brooks run North,
    so I ran North too.
And the white lady helped me
    like she promised she'd do.
The Underground Railroad
    runs out of sight.
The last stop is freedom
    if you ride it right.
Good people gave me food
    and hid me all the way,
until I reached Pennsylvania
    at sunrise one day.
I stared at these black hands
    to make sure I was me.
I felt I was in heaven.
    At last, I was free!

I worked as a cook,
    saved my money
        and then ...
            I went down South
              again and ... again,
leading others to the stations—
    women, children, men.
Yes, I worked and I saved
    and I kept going back.
I never lost a passenger
    or ran my train off the track.

Folks began to call me Moses.
    How the thought tickled me.
No one called him a conductor,
but he set God's children free.

AMERICAN HISTORY POEMS
Scholastic Professional Books, 1998

Freedom!

The Underground Railroad

Most passengers on the Underground Railroad had one-way tickets—north to freedom! But not Harriet Tubman. She made 19 round trips, first returning to Maryland for her family and then venturing into the other slave states. Using the "stations" of the Underground Railroad, she guided over 300 slaves north to freedom. Tubman carried a pistol to threaten runaways who might be tempted to turn back, as well as special herbs to quiet down young children. Between trips Tubman worked hard to save money and didn't hesitate to ask for help from both blacks and whites who ran the "stations." The poem uses some of her own words from an interview with another escaped slave, Frederick Douglass.

Slave holders offered a reward of $40,000 for Tubman "dead or alive." But she was never caught. As a Union scout in 1863, she guided 300 black troops on a raid up the Combahee River. They destroyed a huge cache of Confederate supplies and freed nearly 800 slaves. When Harriet Tubman died in 1916, she was buried with full military honors.

VOCABULARY

Underground Railroad: network of people and places that helped runaway slaves to escape to freedom in the North or Canada

Discussion Question Harriet Tubman was extremely courageous. In spite of the constant threat of being captured "dead or alive," she continued guiding slaves to freedom. Ask students to share times when they have had to act courageously.

Writing Prompt William Still was a black conductor who recorded the stories of every fugitive who passed through his line. One turned out to be his brother. Have the class read about escaping slaves and write a poem or story about a real or fictional runaway from the runaway's point of view.

Extension Activity Have students research the many different routes used on the Underground Railroad. Have them use yarn or string to show the routes on the maps. Then have them calculate the length of each route.

At the Station

Charlene Doolittle: Columbus, Ohio, February, 1861

I

People have been waiting since early in the day.
A train is taking Honest Abe each mile of the way—
All the way from Springfield to Washington, D.C.
President Lincoln! Soon that's who he will be!

With bread and butter sandwiches—Mama in her shawl—
we climbed up a wood pile, being careful not to fall.
"From up here," said Papa, "we're sure to have a view."
We waited, waited, waited, while the crowd grew and grew.

I was glad I had that comforter I didn't want to take.
Our bread and butter sandwiches tasted just like cake.
We waited, waited, waited through that chilly afternoon.
Then that distant whistle—Abe's train was coming soon!

As it pulled into the station, brass bands struck up a song.
Marshals tried to clear a way among the cheering throng.
The crowd began to push, to press, to jostle and to shove.
Papa lifted me so high that I could see Abe from above.

The tall man in a stovepipe hat, smiled when he saw me.
President Lincoln!
        Soon that's who he would be.

Charlene Doolittle: Columbus, Ohio, May, 1865

II

People have been waiting, as night replaces day.
A train is taking Honest Abe each mile of the way—
All the way to Springfield from Washington, D.C.
Rolling back to Illinois…and into history.
Bells are tolling, tolling, tolling, while the wheels click-clack.
For miles beyond the station, people wait along the track.
No brass band stands ready to play a marching song.
No one cheers or pushes as the train rolls along.
The crowd is sad and silent. Some weep quietly.
And I cry for the man in a stovepipe hat…
once he smiled at me.

At the Station

President Abraham Lincoln:

An Instrument of the People

When Lincoln was elected president, he set off for the nation's capital from Springfield, Illinois. His train made "whistle stops" along the way. Lincoln greeted the crowds and attended special receptions in many major cities. Meanwhile, South Carolina had seceded, and Jefferson Davis became the president of the independent confederacy. Many Americans were impressed that the new president was a self-made man. He had been born in a log cabin in Kentucky and spent his childhood on the Illinois frontier. Although he had little schooling, Lincoln read nearly every book he could find. Later he became a successful lawyer. As a politician, Lincoln combined an unaffected style and homespun wit with fairness and political realism.

In the four years between Lincoln's first inauguration and his death, the United States was ripped apart by civil war. But the nation's love for its leader persevered. Over six million Americans of every race and religion came to pay their final respects to him. Most of them waited along the railroad tracks, as a train slowly took his body back to Illinois, retracing almost the same route that had brought Honest Abe to Washington.

VOCABULARY

marshal: an officer in charge of a special ceremony or parade

stovepipe hat: a man's tall silk hat

Discussion Question While he didn't like his nickname Honest Abe, Lincoln certainly earned it. A brilliant lawyer, he usually won his court cases. Yet he did his best to help his clients settle their problems without going to court. Ask the class to think of the nicknames of celebrities or people they know. Then have them discuss how well they think the names describe the people.

Writing Prompt Ask students to pretend that they are newspaper reporters during the 1860s. Have them prepare and perform an interview with Abraham Lincoln after he has been elected president of the United States.

Extension Activity Abraham Lincoln wrote some of the most famous speeches in American history. Have students find copies of his Gettysburg Address or his second inaugural address. After they've read them and discussed them, encourage students to take turns reading the speeches aloud.

A Bird's-Eye View of the Civil War

Old Abe, the Eagle: Madison, Wisconsin, September, 1864

I was just an eaglet when the Civil War began,
living as a pet with a man called Dan McCann.
Volunteers were needed to form the infantry.
Dan didn't volunteer himself. He volunteered… ME!

The men called me Old Abe, and I've done the best I can
to be a worthy namesake of that brave and honest man.
     Joining the Wisconsin 8th, with my Company—
     I'm carried into battle as their flag flies next to me!
When the bands play marches, I flap and stretch my wings.
But oh, from my high perch, I've seen such dreadful things!
Men boasted to each other, "We'll finish this war fast!"
"They're outnumbered three to one." "Johnny Reb won't last."
"We'll be home by Christmas," that's what so many said.
     By Christmas some were wounded.
        By Christmas some were dead.
Through snow,
     through mud,
        through broiling heat,
men march …
     and then march more…
for the Beast that feasts on human life—
     the Beast called Civil War.

Scholastic Professional Books, 1998

Not satisfied with bullets, the War kills with disease.
Measles, mumps, and typhoid—weapons such as these.
At times my troops go hungry. Rebels capture our supplies.
Yet someone always feeds me—sometimes to my surprise.
When they are short of water, men share canteens with me.
In turn I give them courage and hope for victory.

My head feathers have all turned white. It's 1864.
My Company's being mustered out, although there's still a war.
Half the men I led are dead. Yet I am still alive—
a symbol of the Union, we all helped to survive.

Now I wait to meet the Governor with my friend John Hill.
Will I have a perch in Madison? I suspect I will.

AMERICAN HISTORY POEMS
Scholastic Professional Books, 1998

The Beast Called Civil War

While the two major issues of the Civil War were slavery and states' rights, a growing tide of regionalism set the scene for conflict. The agricultural South, the industrial North, and the expanding West: each had different agendas. By 1860 the traditional political parties—Whigs and Democrats—were so divided that Republican Abraham Lincoln won the presidential election with just 40 percent of the popular vote. South Carolina, which had been secretly stockpiling arms for months, immediately seceded from the Union. By Inauguration Day, six other southern states had joined the Confederacy.

Southern troops were greatly outnumbered by the North, which also had a naval force. But the superiority of the South's generals turned what the North expected to be a three-month engagement into four years of terrible bloodshed and destruction.

After the War, Old Abe, the eagle in the poem, traveled to exhibitions to raise money for the United States Sanitary Commission, which cared for veterans on both sides of the conflict. Thousands of pictures of Old Abe were sold, and his keeper taught him to sign them with a peck of his beak. Old Abe was in demand for increasing public appearances for veteran and political groups, but he was always delighted to return to his comfortable basement home in the Madison Capitol. Old Abe died in 1881.

VOCABULARY

infantry: soldiers trained and equipped to fight on foot

Johnny Reb: name given to a Confederate soldier

muster out: to be discharged or let go from military service

John Hill: soldier from the Wisconsin 8th Regiment

Discussion Question Many Union and Confederate troops had mascots that were supposed to bring good luck. Dogs were the most popular, but soldiers adopted raccoons, badgers, and even bears. During the tedious periods between the terror of battles, men taught their mascots tricks. Mascots raised their spirits. Have students discuss the function that mascots play today.

Writing Prompt The Civil War divided loyalties within families, particularly in the border states. In some families, brothers fought on opposing sides. Even the wife of President Lincoln had three brothers who fought for the South. Have students write a conversation that might have taken place in a family in which one son was a Union soldier and one was a Rebel.

Extension Activity At the beginning of the war, the United States had a regular army of about 16,000 men. Initially, the states recruited and supplied their own volunteers. Twenty-three states stayed with the Union and 11 joined the Confederacy. Ask students to learn about the role their state played in the war. Encourage them to visit their local Historical Society, which is usually a good source for photos, letters, and first-person accounts that will make the experiences of the soldiers and the people at home come to life.

A Letter to China

Kun-Yang Lin: Sierra Nevada, August, 1867

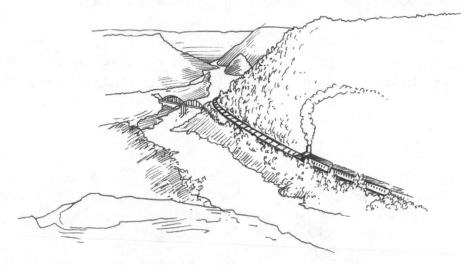

Esteemed Parents:
We hardly know their language—
just their hate and their disgust—
    as we see them sneer
       and we hear them jeer,
keeping silent as we must.

They give us the most dangerous jobs.
Each day we prove our skill.
    They are loud and rough.
       We are quiet…but tough,
bending mountains with sheer will.

They never use our proper names.
We're not men to them, I think.
    We don't show our fright.
       We plant dynamite,
making way for the next rail link.

I am so exhausted, Parents.
Too tired this night to sleep.
But at dawn I'll work with honor
for wages which you must keep.

AMERICAN HISTORY POEMS
Scholastic Professional Books, 1998

A Letter to China

The Iron Road:

The Transcontinental Railroad

After the Civil War, the dream of uniting the country by railroad became a reality. Theodore Judah convinced four Sacramento, California, shopkeepers that it was possible to lay tracks through the ridges and across the ravines of the Sierra Nevada mountains. The Central Pacific Railroad was formed to raise funds and muster congressional support. Finally work began in the West.

In the East, the Union Pacific Railroad started laying track. Civil War veterans and new immigrants—Irish, German, Dutch—did most of the work. In the more sparsely populated West, the Central Pacific faced a shortage of dependable labor. The chief engineer, Charles Crocker, hesitated to recruit Chinese workers. He feared they would not be strong enough for the work. Eventually nine out of ten workers were Chinese. Subject to cruel prejudice and living apart from other workers, the Chinese proved themselves to be the bravest and most dependable soldiers in "Crocker's Army." Lowered over cliffs in woven baskets, they planted dynamite to blast into the rock. They built bridges to span deep chasms. Several thousand Chinese lost their lives building the railroad. Racing against each other, the two lines finally met at Promontory Point, Utah, on May 10, 1869. The whole country celebrated!

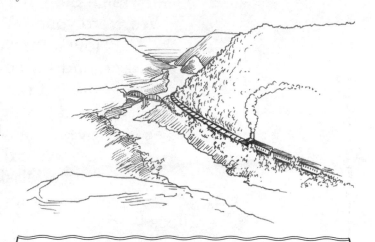

VOCABULARY

esteemed: someone or something that is thought highly of

sneer: to say with or have an expression of the face that shows hatred or scorn

jeer: to make fun of a person

Discussion Question Have students discuss why they think that immigrants like Kun-Yang Lin agreed to take jobs building the railroad.

Writing Prompt Ask students to imagine that they are reporters in the 1860s. Have them write a newspaper story about the completion of the Transcontinental Railroad.

Extension Activity Ask students to create a bulletin board display about the building of the Transcontinental Railroad. Their displays might include maps and drawings as well as copies of popular railroad songs, such as "I've Been Working on the Railroad" and "Wabash Cannonball."

A Pioneer Woman Looks Back

Mary Stahler: Kansas, 1874

"Free for the taking. At that price, you can buy... a garden in the West... endless land and endless sky!"

We were just newlyweds.
John said, "It seems best
to grow with the country—
raise our family out West."
We were young. We were strong.
How were we to know
land and sky could be cruel?
We got ready to go.
I smiled through my tears,
as our loved ones waved good-by.
We crossed
the Mississippi
for
endless land...   endless sky...

The trail was rough
and the going was tough.
The prairies of Kansas
were far West enough.
John staked out our claim
one hot day in July.
As I waited and watched—
endless land...   endless sky...

Young John was born
early that fall.
Next came Mary,
then Elizabeth—
nine kids in all.

AMERICAN HISTORY POEMS
Scholastic Professional Books, 1998

I schooled the children.
Town was too far away.
There were so many chores
to fit into a day!
Cooking, sewing, laundry—
and much more to do.
Yet somehow I found time
to be lonely, too.
The endless droning of the wind,
a lone coyote's call,
the chatter of the children—
no visitors at all.
I longed to see a woman—
to hear a woman's voice.
Instead, I hear winds whisper:
Free land! You made a choice.
Often I wonder,
and I can't help but sigh—
What price we really paid
for
endless land...   endless sky...

A Pioneer Woman Looks Back
Homesteaders!

During the 1840s, fur traders, gold seekers, and pioneer families had been gradually settling the land west of the Mississippi. By 1850 California had become a state. The Homestead Act of 1862 offered free farmland to anyone willing to work it for five years. As a result, families began making the long trek west. By the 1870s and 1880s, an endless line of "prairie schooners"—canvas-covered wagons drawn by patient, powerful oxen—lined the Santa Fe and Oregon trails between May and September.

For some the price of the journey into "the great emptiness" was hardship and heartbreak. Often hard work, sacrifice, and terrible loneliness lay ahead. In well forested areas, pioneers built snug log cabins. In the Kansas grasslands, they usually dug a hole and built sod houses. Water had to be hauled miles before deep wells could be dug. The women gathered buffalo chips for fuel. Everything was in short supply—except land and sky!

VOCABULARY

claim: something that is claimed, such as a piece of land

droning: a low, continuous humming sound

Discussion Question Point out to kids the way the words "endless land" and "endless sky" are spaced in the poem. Why do they think the poet did this?

Writing Prompt Settlers faced terrible winter blizzards, twisters, prairie brush fires, plagues of grasshoppers, and periods of drought and extreme heat. One response was to make up "tall tales"—absurd exaggerations—about the weather. For example: *It was so hot, all the corn growing in my field started popping. My horse thought it was a blizzard, lay down, and froze to death.* Invite students to write and illustrate their own tall tales.

Extension Activity Some of the earlier pioneers published guides with advice for those to come. Suggest that students work in small groups to collaborate on a guidebook with helpful tips for newcomers to your area.

AMERICAN HISTORY POEMS
Scholastic Professional Books, 1998

A Useless Gadget

A conversation between Gardner Green Hubbard and Thomas Sanders:
Boston, Massachusetts, May 31, 1875

He is such a brilliant fellow—
Alexander Graham Bell.

> *But the gadget which intrigues him*
> *sometimes makes that hard to tell.*

I wish he'd do something useful
and leave that thing alone.

> *He wastes our money tinkering.*
> *Who needs a telephone?*

A conversation between Thomas Watson and Alexander Graham Bell:
Boston, Massachusetts, March 10, 1876

Shall we try the new transmitter?
I finished it last night.

> *The sound should be better,*
> *if we've gotten things right.*

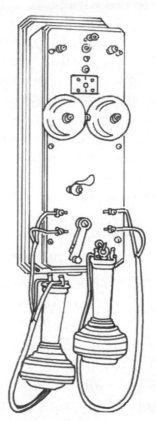

We'll know when we test it.
Let's do what we have to do.

> *Mr. Watson, come here.*
> *I want you!*

A Useless Gadget

Number, Please! The Telephone

Although Alexander Graham Bell (1847-1922) was a musical genius, he chose to study vocal anatomy. He hoped to advance his work of helping the deaf to speak. Young Bell came to the United States to open a school for teachers of the deaf and soon became a professor at Boston University. Gardner Green Hubbard and Thomas Sanders consulted him about their deaf children. When they learned that Bell was conducting electrical experiments in his spare time, they gave him money to finance his research. But, as the poem reveals, they were not too pleased with how he was spending their funds. Bell had hired an electrician, Thomas Watson, to fabricate parts for his "gadget," which was based on the technology of the telegraph. The last two lines of the poem are the first spoken words carried by a telephone wire!

When Bell demonstrated his newly patented telephone at the Centennial Exhibi-tion in 1876, an English scientist described it as "the most wonderful thing in America." The next year, the Bell Telephone Company began offering service. Several years later, Bell helped establish the Volta Laboratory for furthering research to aid the deaf. Among the variety of inventions developed at Volta was a method to capture sound on wax discs—the phonograph record.

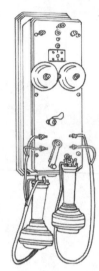

VOCABULARY

tinker: to make clumsy or useless attempts to mend or repair something

transmitter: a device that sends out radio signals

Discussion Question Alexander Graham Bell was interested in aviation his whole life and spent years experimenting with flight. He organized the Aerial Experiment Association in 1907. Yet he is remembered for the telephone. Ask the class to discuss whether the telephone or the airplane has changed people's lives more.

Writing Prompt In these days of cellular phones, answering machines, and Fax machines, we take the telephone for granted. Have the class write a play in which all phone services throughout the world are stopped for a day.

Extension Activity Before direct dialing was started, people needed operators to put through their calls. Not everyone could afford a phone, and many people had "party lines" as opposed to private ones. Corner candy stores and upstairs neighbors took messages for people without phones. Have students interview senior citizens about the days when picking up a receiver meant hearing an operator say, "Number, please."

Will We Be a New State?

Lizzy Bonneville: Laramie, Wyoming Territory, May 7, 1888

We became a Territory
back in 1868.
Now Wyoming's asking Congress
to accept us as a State.
"We won't come in without our women!"
That's the message from Cheyenne.
(To vote in any other State,
you have to be a man.)

My granny cast a ballot,
almost twenty years ago.
Women judges in Wyoming
show they know what they should know.
So when they see our Constitution
in Washington, D.C.,
they will see a plank protecting
voting rights for Mom and me.
That could cause a royal rumpus
and a whirlwind of debate.
But…
if they won't let our women vote,
Wyoming *won't* become a State.

Will We Be a New State?

The Growth of a Nation:

Adding a Star to the Flag

One by one, huge territories west of the Mississippi were divided into somewhat smaller units. (Wyoming Territory originally consisted of parts of Utah, Idaho, and Dakota.) First these units applied for status as official United States territories. After the president appointed a governor, the people elected a legislature, which in turn drafted a state constitution and eventually petitioned for statehood.

The United States Constitution limited voters to males, but when Wyoming became an official territory women were granted the right to vote. The first governor appointed women judges, who became "the terror of all rogues...." Women began to serve on juries. Cynics accused Wyoming of using women's rights as a publicity stunt to attract new settlers, but 20 years later the state's sincerity was clear.

In 1888 Wyoming hoped to become a state, but its citizens were unwilling to sacrifice women's rights to win acceptance. And they prevailed! On July 10, 1890, Wyoming became the 44th state in the Union.

VOCABULARY

Cheyenne: capital of Wyoming

rumpus: a noisy or violent disturbance

Discussion Question   Encourage the class to discuss why they think people on the frontier were more democratic than those living along the East coast.

Writing Prompt   Ask students to imagine that they are newspaper reporters in Wyoming in 1890. Have them write a newspaper story about Wyoming's becoming a state.

Extension Activity   When did African-American men gain the right to vote? When did 18-year-olds first begin voting? When did women? Ask students to create a timeline on a bulletin board showing the history of voting rights in the United States. Be sure they include names, dates, and the numbers of those constitutional amendments that apply.

A Matter of Life or . . . Death

Jake Kahn: Chicago, 1893

Mama, Papa, I'll *die* if we don't go.
We *have* to see
Bill Cody's Wild West Show!
Folks say that you've
never
ever
really had a thrill
until you've seen the likes
of Buffalo Bill.
Annie Oakley, Little Sure Shot—
she's sure to be there—
putting holes through playing cards
tossed up in the air!
Forty, fifty cowboys—daredevils all—
ride faster than tornadoes
and NEVER take a fall!
Arapahoe, Shoshone, Chiefs of the Sioux,
calf ropers, bulldoggers—
they'll be there, too!
The Deadwood stagecoach,
the Pony Express—
You want to see them.
Don't you? Confess!
With thousands of seats, the tickets don't last.
We better get there fast, fast, fast!
Mama, Papa, I'll *die* if we don't go.
We *have* to see
Bill Cody's Wild West Show!

A Matter of Life or . . . Death

Cowhands and Legends of the Wild West

About three million longhorn cattle were roaming the grasslands of southern Texas at the end of the Civil War. The longhorns sold for about $4 a head. In eastern cities, however, where beef was in demand, buyers would pay up to $40 for each animal. The problem was how to get the longhorns to eastern markets. The coming of the railroad gave Joseph McCoy, a livestock trader from Chicago, an idea: bring the longhorns to large cattle pens in central Kansas. Then ship them by rail to markets across the country. McCoy bought the tiny town of Abilene, Kansas, for $5 an acre, and recruited cowhands to drive the cattle there from Texas. The result was the Chisolm Trail and the start of a legend that has lasted to this day. Abilene became a rough and violent town—with saloons, gambling parlors, and marshals like "Wild Bill Hickok," enforcing the law with six-shooters.

The actual era of cattle drives was very short. The invention of barbed wire and the introduction of Angus and Hereford cattle made ranching more profitable. But the golden age of the cowhand captured the imagination of the nation. Rodeos, circuses, and "Wild West" Shows— none better known than Buffalo's Bill's crowd-thrilling extravaganzas— kept the legend alive. The Chicago Exposition of 1893 marked the 400th anniversary of Columbus's arrival in America. When planners turned down Buffalo Bill's request to take part in the celebrations, he built a grandstand to seat 18,000 people across from the fairgrounds. Tickets were completely sold out day after day.

VOCABULARY

bulldogger: someone who throws a bull by taking hold of its horns and twisting its neck

---

Discussion Question Encourage the class to discuss why life in frontier towns such as Abilene was often so rough.

Writing Prompt Have students try to find out more about rodeos. Ask them to choose one rodeo event to describe in detail.

Extension Activity Longhorns were wild and nervous animals. While we may consider songs such as "Home on the Range" or "The Old Chisolm Trail" as romantic, they were really lullabies that cowhands crooned to calm down the longhorns. Have the class learn the words and melody of one of these songs. Let them work in small groups to perform their songs with appropriate gestures.

A Gold Miner's Tale

Frank Wexler: Dawson City, Yukon Territory, 1898

I was twenty-one years old.
Fired up by dreams of gold.
    Rushing West in '49,
        to stake a claim to my own mine!
           What did I find when I got there?
             Thousands of "Rushers" everywhere!
    Water and sand. That's all it takes.
    Swish your pan. Pick out the flakes!
A meal?
    A horse?
        A place to stay?
Who'd believe what we had to pay!

Bought a shovel. Bought a pan.
Soon I'd be a rich young man.
    Water and sand. That's all it takes.
    Swish your pan. Pick out the flakes!
But working a placer,
    you need luck.
        One pan has flakes.
           Fifty others just muck.
Pan after pan, I'd swish and wish
for the glint of pay dirt in my dish.
Asleep at night, what did I see?
Nuggets the daylight hid from me.
It takes more than a flash in the pan
to make a rusher a rich young man.

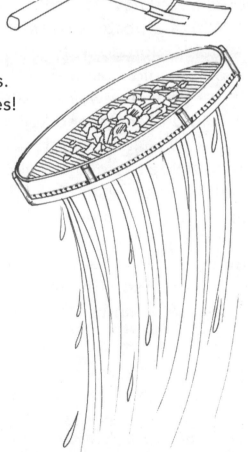

The gold I found? Just enough to get by.
I gave up, when my claim went dry.
     Water and sand. That's all it takes.
     Swish your pan. Pick out the flakes!

Got a job in a hydraulic mine.
Hated the work, but the pay was fine.
So when I heard about Pikes Peak,
     I

          was

               in

                    the Rockies
                       within a week!
Water and sand. That's all it takes.
Swish your pan. Pick out the flakes!
I should have known better.
     With a grubstake so small,
     I left Colorado with nothing at all.
No job. No gold. Just a shovel and a pan.
     But I walked away a wiser man.
     "Gold in the Klondike!"
          Wouldn't you think
     I'd be up there in a wink?
But with my new plan to pan gold flakes,
I didn't make the same mistakes.
Before I joined the great stampede,
I thought: What will stampeders need?
Now I'm a Dawson City millionaire!
I sell them ALL long underwear.

AMERICAN HISTORY POEMS
Scholastic Professional Books, 1998

A Gold Miner's Tale

The Rush for Gold!

In America nothing seemed to ignite the spirit of adventure and opportunity more than the magic word—gold. Racing from strike to strike, from boom to bust, most prospectors, like Frank Wexler, were lucky if they found even a thimbleful of gold a day.

In 1849 over 70,000 people left their homes for California in search of gold. By 1860, $595 million dollars worth of gold had been found. By 1900 the Sierra Nevadas yielded $700 million more. The gold rush population soared to 380,000 in just 12 years!

In 1858 a small find in the Rocky Mountains was blown out of proportion by journalists. "Gold is found everywhere you stick your shovel" claimed one newspaper. By the following year, with signs saying PIKES PEAK OR BUST, over 100,000 prospectors set off, many of them ill-prepared novices from the East. Confused and lost, more than a few died from thirst, disease, or attacks by Plains Indians. Most headed for home with signs saying BUSTED, BY GOSH.

A few lucky miners did find gold in Colorado. Some even made fabulous fortunes overnight, which allowed them to develop deep mines or invest in new businesses. For example, Silver King John Mackay sold out his interest in the Comstock Mine and organized a cable company that laid wire across the Atlantic and Pacific oceans. Still others, like Frank Wexler, became wealthy by supplying miners with tools, clothing, and lodging.

VOCABULARY

claim: an area of land in a gold field that a prospector, or person looking for gold or other minerals, had staked out and registered

placer: a deposit of gravel or sand along streams or rivers that contains gold; the gold has been eroded from its original rock and is concentrated in small particles that can be washed out

pay dirt: gold left in the pan after washing

flash in the pan: mica and certain other minerals that flash like gold in the sunlight

hydraulic: something that is operated by the movement and force of liquid

grubstake: the money or supplies advanced to a prospector in return for a share of his findings

Discussion Question In 1849 and again in 1859, Americans searched hungrily for gold, hoping to strike it rich. Ask students to discuss one or two ways in which people today might try to make a quick fortune.

Writing Prompt Have students find out more about the Klondike gold rush. Then ask them to write a report about what happened to most prospectors there.

Extension Activity Miners paid for their purchases in gold, which they weighed on tiny pocket scales. One man carried crates full of cats over the treacherous trails. He sold each one for an ounce of gold to the lonely miners. More people got rich from selling gold seekers what they needed than from finding gold. Have students try to find out what things cost in Dawson City in 1898.

America!

Fanya Albert: Ellis Island, March 7, 1911

Soon the Golden Land would welcome them,
the first-class passengers,
the ones with cabins.
From behind the metal gate,
I could glimpse fragments:
            a billowing feather on a hat,
      a silk scarf,
                  a tapered hand in pale suede,
            an elegant carrying case.
They would go straight to the city.

Not us. Not the steerage.
            Feathers?
Ours, if any, had been sewn into quilts.
We had no suede gloves,
            no silk—
just babushkas and bundles,
hopes and prayers.
First we must go to Ellis Island.

We waited.
A human jumble:
babies crying, elders sighing,
our ears swimming in a noisy stew
of German, Italian, Swedish, Yiddish,
even English with an Irish lilt.
We did not understand each others' words,
except one—
America!

AMERICAN HISTORY POEMS
Scholastic Professional Books, 1998

At last the gate swung open,
and we crowded into the ferry.
Then, as it pulled away from the ship,
we saw her—Lady Liberty!
A goddess
rising from the sea,
her strong arm holding a torch
as if to light our way.
One by one we whispered the word,
     "America!"
          "America!"
Again and again,
          "America!"
     "America!"
until
     the echoed word became a blizzard!
A swarm of sparkling jewels that I could see
          hovering
     over the dark water.

Minutes later,
the ferry docked at Ellis Island.
Looking at us,
a worn and shabby crowd,
could anyone tell?
Could anyone know
we each carried a treasure?
It was a single precious word—
     America!

America!

Ellis Island:

An Isle of Hope, an Isle of Tears

During the 19th century, immigration to the United States gained momentum. Better equipped packet ships carried the wealthier passengers to America. Most immigrants, however, were prey for greedy ship owners who jammed them into the holds of sailing ships, where they traveled in such deplorable conditions that illness, and even death, were not uncommon. When Congress finally passed the U.S. Passenger Act, which set standards for ventilation, deck space, and other facilities, the law did not include incoming vessels—nor any enforcement procedure! As steamships, first of iron and then of steel, replaced sailing ships, immigrants were the last ones to benefit from improved safety and shorter voyages.

Between 1860 and 1920, 28.5 million people left Europe and Asia to come to the United States. Most of them passed through the federal immigration station in New York Harbor, which was opened in 1892. Its name, Ellis Island, was engraved in the memories of all who stopped there. For most, it was an Isle of Hope. For others, who did not pass the demanding physical, it was an Isle of Tears for they were sent back home. First-class and cabin-class passengers were given superficial examinations by a public-health doctor and inspector who boarded the arriving ships. They were permitted to go directly to New York City. Steerage passengers, like Fanya Albert, were herded onto ferries that took them to Ellis Island.

VOCABULARY

steerage: section in some ships occupied by passengers paying the lowest fare

babushka: a scarf worn on the head by a girl or woman and tied under the chin

lilt: a light, swingy, and graceful rhythm

Discussion Question Encourage students to discuss why newcomers like Fanya Albert saw America as a land of opportunity.

Writing Prompt Read the class the following lines from the sonnet by Emma Lazarus, which is now on plaques at the Statue of Liberty and the International Arrivals Building at Kennedy International Airport:

"…Give me your tired, your poor,
your huddled masses yearning to breathe free,
    The wretched refuse of your teeming shore,

Send these, the tempest-tossed to me,
    I lift my lamp beside the golden door!"

Ask students to write poems from the point of view of an immigrant arriving in America.

Extension Activity Have students work in pairs to conduct a pretend interview of an immigrant arriving in the United States. One student should come up with a list of questions to ask about the immigration experience. The other student should try to respond to the questions as if he or she were actually an immigrant.

A Song for Suffrage

Virginia Duncan: Trenton, New Jersey, February, 1913

(To the tune of "The Battle Hymn of the Republic")

We are marching, marching, marching
    off to Washington, D.C.,
With a message for the President,
    whom we intend to see.
Men claim that they adore us!
    "Voting would be such a strain."
So we're marching, marching, marching,
    but we might melt in the rain!

Chorus: Women, we've been told it's fitting
    to stay home and do our knitting.
    But we're determined. We're not quitting.
    Won't you march with us today?

We're soldiers in the Women's Army.
    Sisters, come along, enlist.
We'll never get the right to vote,
    unless we all insist.
You can march with us for one mile.
    You can march with us for ten.
As we march to the Potomac
    for the right to vote like men!

Chorus: Women, we've been told it's fitting
    to stay home and do our knitting.
    But we're determined. We're not quitting.
    Won't you march with us today?

AMERICAN HISTORY POEMS
Scholastic Professional Books, 1998

Men say they wish to protect us,
    and proceed to show us how.
They can take away our children
    the way laws are written now.
They are ready to protect us
    from our fathers' tyranny
By controlling what Dad leaves us
    to make sure we're worry-free!

Chorus: Women, we've been told it's fitting
    to stay home and do our knitting.
    But we're determined. We're not quitting.
    Won't you march with us today?

AMERICAN HISTORY POEMS
Scholastic Professional Books, 1998

A Song for Suffrage

Women Win the Right to Vote

The Susan B. Anthony Suffrage Amendment was first introduced in Congress in 1878, but it was not passed until 1919—41 years later. While some states had granted women voting rights earlier, the 19th Amendment finally granted women the right to vote in national elections. Although the name Susan B. Anthony has become synonymous with women's suffrage, she was just one of many Americans who believed that women were entitled to vote. For example, former slaves such as Frederick Douglass and Sojourner Truth campaigned for equal rights for *all* Americans well before the Civil War. Abigail Adams, the wife of John Adams, had reminded him "to remember the ladies" when he was attending the Continental Congress in 1776. And, in 1866, Peter Wilson, Chief of the Seneca, urged white men to follow the tradition of *his* nation by sharing voting rights with women. However, when the 14th and 15th amendments were passed, in 1868 and 1869 respectively, they extended the protection of Constitutional and voting rights to ALL— men.

VOCABULARY

enlist: to join a group, such as the army, navy, or some other part of the armed forces

tyranny: the cruel use of force or authority

Discussion Question Today millions of women hold jobs outside the home. But they often don't receive pay equal to that of men holding the same job. Encourage the class to discuss the issue of equal pay for work of comparable worth.

Writing Prompt Have students write a biographical report about one of the leaders of the American suffrage movement. They might consider Susan B. Anthony, Mary Ann Shad, Sojourner Truth, or Carrie Chapman Catt.

Extension Activity Women sang songs as they marched from New York City to Washington, D.C., to dramatize their cause and enlist support. Thousands of women joined the marchers along the route for several miles or more. Fourteen suffragettes walked the full distance, about 300 miles. Have students sing along with Virginia Duncan and try adding a verse of their own. Then have them research any other songs that women sang as they marched together in suffrage parades.

The Assembly Line

Billy Berman: Highland Park, Michigan, January, 1914

Five dollars a day!
    Five dollars a day!
Mr. Ford went and doubled
    my papa's pay!
What's more on the Ford
    assembly line,
the hours are cut back
    to eight from nine!
Papa used to complain all that he got to do

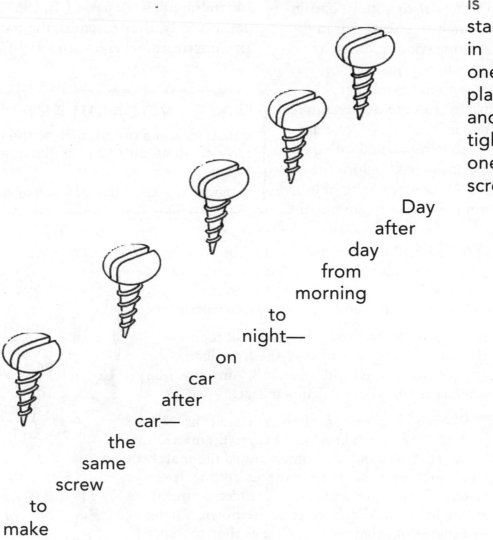

is
stand
in
one
place
and
tighten
one
screw.
Day
after
day
from
morning
to
night—
on
car
after
car—
the
same
screw
to
make
tight.

AMERICAN HISTORY POEMS
Scholastic Professional Books, 1998

"We're putting together the Model T,
but the screw I turn is all I see.
Each man works in such little bits.
Soon all of us will lose our wits!
The belt speeds up. We must work faster.
Are we still men, when Time's our master?"

But now that he's getting twice the pay,
      Here's what I hear Papa say:
      Five dollars a day!
            Five dollars a day!
The
a
s
s
e
m
b
l
y
l
i
n
e
 is
  here
 to
 stay
  !

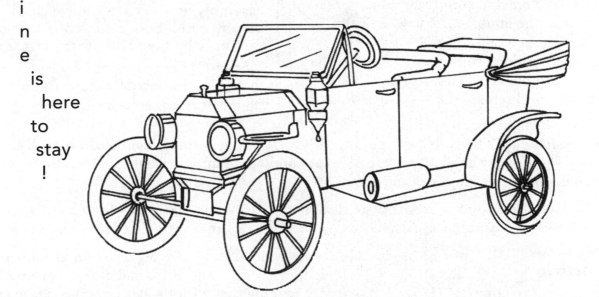

The Assembly Line
The Model "T":
Mass Production for Mass Consumption

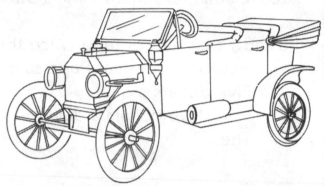

Development of the first "horseless carriage," which appeared in the 19th century, was sidetracked by excitement over train travel. By the turn of the century, however, various types of automobiles were on the market in Europe and the United States. Whether powered by steam, electricity, or the internal combustion engine, they were merely expensive toys for the rich.

Henry Ford decided to manufacture a "universal car," a rugged, simple vehicle that most Americans could afford. To do so, he applied the most advanced technology to a much older principle: mass production. The result was the Model "T." Each year it cost less to produce the car. A percentage of the savings and profits were shared by consumers and workers alike. In 1913 the Ford plant produced over 250,000 Model "T"s. Henry Ford created an international sensation, when he doubled the pay of skilled workers from $2.50 to $5.00 a day and unskilled workers from $1.00 to $2.00. The next year productivity increased to 300,000 cars, and Ford refunded $50.00 to anyone who had purchased a car the previous year. The lowest price, $260, was reached in 1925. Between 1908 and 1927, 15 million Model "T"s rolled off the assembly line at the 60-acre plant that Ford had built in Highland Park. The days of the horse and buggy were ending at last.

VOCABULARY

assembly line: a system in which a conveyor belt brings parts of a product to workers who then add other parts to it

Model "T": car produced by Henry Ford that was affordable by many people

Discussion Question Be sure to point out the format of the poem. Encourage kids to discuss how the words in the poem are broken up into lines and angles. How does this spacing reflect the subject of the poem?

Writing Prompt Ask students to pretend that it's 1913 and that they work on an assembly line producing cars. Have them write a journal entry describing one day at work.

Extension Activity Limiting production to one basic model was a big factor in keeping car prices down. Have students visit car dealerships and observe print and TV ads in order to compare Henry Ford's way of making cars with today's methods. Have students work in pairs to conduct a survey by asking ten drivers the following question: Would you prefer automobile manufacturers to offer fewer models of cars if that made prices lower? Students should report their findings to the rest of the class.

A New Deal: That's What the Country Needs

Franklin Delano Roosevelt: Chicago, Illinois, July, 1932

The people I call Americans,
Hoover calls "the mob."
Can this be democracy?
The people are no mob to me.
I have met them face to face:
       the factory worker,
       the farmer,
       the miner,
       the veteran,
       the woman, so lean, so worried,
       the hungry children—
       whose schools have been closed,
       the elderly—
       with fear in their eyes.
They are the forgotten Americans,
the ones without the cards it takes to win.
So let us shuffle the deck
and restore their country to its own people
with...
       a new deal.

A New Deal: That's What the Country Needs

FDR:

The President with an Alphabet of Answers

Franklin Delano Roosevelt was the governor of New York in 1929, when the stock market suddenly crashed, wiping out the earnings of investors and stock brokers. The economy went into a downward spiral. Workers were laid off or fired; farmers couldn't get fair prices for their produce; people lost their homes and life savings. Shantytowns of the homeless sprang up all over the country. Cities and towns went bankrupt. Schools began to close. Governor Roosevelt appealed to the legislature to raise taxes to start a Temporary Relief Administration—the first such program in the country—and to create jobs with public works and land reclamation projects. He fought for farmers facing mortgage foreclosures and for regulation of utilities. Using the radio, Roosevelt began a series of "Fireside Chats" to explain his programs in terms that people could understand.

When Roosevelt became the Democratic candidate in 1934, he promised a "New Deal" to restore America to its own people. His campaign train, the "Roosevelt Special," traveled 27,000 miles—all over the country. The widespread suffering and mounting anger he saw convinced him that only bold new plans could save democracy. His optimistic attitude gave the country new hope.

VOCABULARY

veteran: a person who has served in the armed forces

Discussion Question Roosevelt was struck by poliomyelitis in 1921. He was determined not to remain helpless, even though he would have to wear leg braces and use crutches for the rest of his life. His friend Louis Howe wrote that while he was "flat on his back…his horizon widened…he thought of others who were ill…and in want. Lying there, he grew bigger day by day." Ask the class to discuss whether disabilities can sometimes make people stronger and kinder.

Writing Prompt Eleanor Roosevelt was a new breed of First Lady. She traveled all over the country, meeting people and learning about their problems and working conditions. She wrote a newspaper column, "My Day." She helped FDR feel the pulse of the people. Have the class write one or two paragraphs about the role of the current First Lady in the life of the nation.

Extension Activity On Election Day, 1932, there were 14 million unemployed Americans. By the time Roosevelt took office in 1933, there were 16 million. He started programs that not only put people back to work but also improved the country in many ways. Have teams of students report on the Civilian Conservation Corps (CCC), the National Youth Administration (NYA), the Works Progress Administration (WPA) or the Tennessee Valley Authority (TVA). Ask students to find out whether one of these programs brought a park, road, ranger station, hospital, or some other improvement to your area.

On the Way to Californ-I-A!

Everett Dansby: Mother Road, Oklahoma, 1938

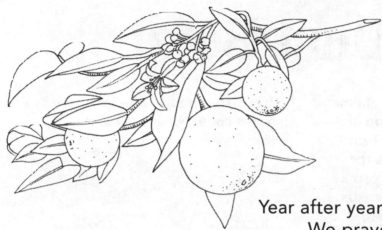

Year after year, the land was dry.
We prayed for rain—
watched crops shrivel and die.
Then the winds started blowing,
and the sky turned blood red.
But no raindrops fell.
It rained red dust, instead.
The sun disappeared.
Day turned into night.
We rushed inside.
Tried to make the house tight.
And the terror winds blew and blew and blew.
And the terror winds blew and blew.

"There's jobs in Californ-I-A!"
That's what Pa says folks say.
So we loaded our jalopy,
and we're on our way today!
On our way to Californ-I-A
where
oranges,
tomatoes,
and potatoes grow—
and where
terror winds don't ever blow.
No, the terror winds don't blow.

On the Way to Californ-I-A!

The Great Depression and the Dust Bowl

For the small farmers of the Oklahoma Panhandle, the Great Depression of 1929 meant lower grain prices. Families were forced to borrow money from the bank in order to buy seed for the next year's crop. Then in 1931 nature added its own disaster—five years with little or no rain. In 1936, the wind started to blow—harder and harder—for four long years. The wind blew down barns and buried farm animals. It carried away all the topsoil, leaving acres of red clay and creating a huge dust bowl.

Hungry and penniless, drawn by ads promising work for good pay, many people set off for California. Over one million men, women, and children poured into the state between 1935 and 1940—the largest migration this country has ever seen.

VOCABULARY

jalopy: an old, rickety automobile

Discussion Question Encourage students to discuss how the climate and landscape of the Great Plains contributed to the Dust Bowl. Ask students how the location of their hometown affects the climate there.

Writing Prompt Have students pretend that their families were farmers on the Great Plains during the Great Depression. Then ask them to write a short story, poem, or skit in which they show how the dust storms affected them.

Extension Activity Have students look at a map of the Great Plains. Point out that the Panhandle is sandwiched between Texas, Kansas, Colorado, and New Mexico. Have students find this area on the map and decide if the name fits. Then ask them to name which states were part of the Dust Bowl.

Shopping

Liza Charlesworth: San Jose, California, 1940

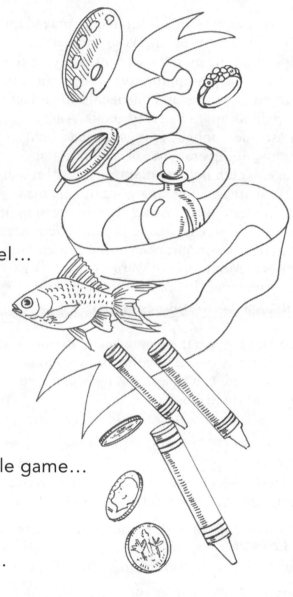

Five pennies make a nickel.
      Two nickels make a dime.
A dime can buy a treasure
      at Woolworth's every time.
Silk and velvet ribbons…
      a tortoise-shell barrette…
          perfume for my mother…
              a water-color set…
      a whirling, twirling pinwheel…
jacks…
a ruby ring…
I study every counter
      before I choose a thing.
A hankie with the letter *L*
      the way I start my name…
          new crayons…
              jigsaw puzzles…
                a ball and paddle game…
If I only had permission,
      my dime could buy a pet—
          a tiny painted turtle…
      goldfish scooped up with a net…
But sometimes,
      only sometimes,
I save my dime
      and then…
I think of how I'll spend it,
      when I come back again.

Shopping the American Way

Although railroads often encouraged the settlement of the West, the cost of shipping by rail was constantly on the rise. Eventually shipping costs ate up most of the farmers' profits and pushed up the prices they paid for manufactured goods. Angry homesteaders sought to organize and fight back by joining branches of the National Grange, which held regular meetings throughout rural areas. Soon Grange members made an agreement with a traveling sales person, or drummer, from Chicago to provide them with any items they might need at fair prices. His name was Montgomery Ward. In 1872 he gave them a one-page list of his offerings. By 1875 his list had grown into a seventy-two-page illustrated catalog. And it's been growing ever since. In 1886 what became Sears, Roebuck and Company began to compete with Montgomery Ward. Catalog shopping became an American tradition.

As the 20th century progressed, department stores and specialty shops lined main streets in cities throughout the country. But perhaps none held quite as much allure for children as the chain of " five-cent," and then "five-and-ten" stores started by Frank W. Woolworth in 1880. By 1934 Woolworth's raised its top prices to 20 cents. Although the price ceiling was eventually eliminated, prices remained very low through the 1950s. By 1960 Woolworth's sales were over $1 billion. Discount stores, convenience stores, and shopping malls, gradually made the stores unprofitable. The last Woolworth's shut its doors in 1997.

VOCABULARY

Woolworth's: a store which originally sold many items for only 5 or 10 cents

---

Discussion Question Catalog shopping is an American invention. The frontier made it a necessity. Now there are shopping channels on television and an increased number of specialized catalogs. Encourage students to discuss why, with all the retail stores, Americans still use alternative methods of shopping.

Writing Prompt Ask students what they can buy with a dime today. Which items in the poem would be dificult to find? Have them write one or two paragraphs describing the kinds of things they like to shop for.

Extension Activity The 1908 Sears catalog offers a Beckwith piano for a bargain price of $87.00; road wagons start at $25.95 and go all the way up to $104.95 for the "Solid Comfort" family surrey. These are just samples of what you'll find in the 1,184-page catalog. Mail order catalogs are wonderful documents of an era. Have students work in teams to create a "catalog" of current day America. They should cut out ads from newspapers and sales fliers showing clothing, toys, sporting goods, cars, tools, musical instruments, home furnishings, and electronic equipment. Have students group the ads by categories before rewriting the descriptions. Finally they should mount the pictures, prices, and descriptions on plain paper and gather them together.

AMERICAN HISTORY POEMS
Scholastic Professional Books, 1998

On the Home Front

Gina Shaw: San Antonio, Texas, September, 1942

Victor Frager's wearing silver wings.
  Walter Dodge is a marine;
Cousin Sonny's in the army
  with a rifle to keep clean.
Tony Vacca joined the navy.
  Steve Smith's in the Signal Corps.
Jane Finnegan's become a WAC.
  The whole world is at war.

We're busy on the home front,
  doing all that we can do.
We save every bit of tinfoil
  from each stick of gum we chew.
Like our rubber-band collection,
  it gets added to a ball.
Our school principal has told us,
  "The war effort needs it all."
During art class we're all knitting
  squares that someone else will sew
into blankets that are shipped off
  to wherever they should go.
During English we write letters
  so that G.I.s know we care,
and we feel their boundless courage,
  while we're singing "Over There!"

Neighbors work in Victory Gardens
  in backyards along our street.
We have books of ration coupons
  to buy butter, sugar, meat.
Every evening my whole family
  sits close to the radio.
Are the Allied troops advancing?
  What's the news? We have to know.

Uncle Sam peers down from posters,
  and he's saying, "I need you!"
I think and think and think and think
  what can I really do.
Watching newsreels at the movies,
  I think and think some more.
And I wonder—Will peace *ever* come?
  The whole world is at war.

AMERICAN HISTORY POEMS
Scholastic Professional Books, 1998

On the Home Front

World War II:

Uncle Sam Needs You!

As Franklin Delano Roosevelt became president in 1933 with a vision of democracy, Europe was heading in a very different direction. Adolf Hitler became chancellor of Germany with a plan for world conquest by the "master race." He moved quickly and ruthlessly to establish a Nazi dictatorship and build a powerful army, fomenting hatred against Jews and Communists. In Italy, the fascist dictator, Benito Mussolini, came to power, while in Spain, Francisco Franco overthrew the democratic republic of Spain. On the other side of the world, Japan occupied Korea and much of China.

In the years that followed, Germany gobbled up country after country—Poland, Holland, Denmark, Norway—with "blitzkrieg" (lightning) attacks. In the East, Japan occupied China and French Indochina—Vietnam, Cambodia, Laos. Any American who was old enough at the time will never forget the

Japanese attack on Pearl Harbor, Hawaii, on December 7, 1941. Over 2,400 Americans were killed, 19 battleships were sunk, and over 150 planes were demolished. The next day Congress united behind FDR and declared war on Japan. Across the Atlantic, Britain did likewise. It took only three days for Germany and Italy to declare war on the United States.

VOCABULARY

Signal Corps: the part of an army in charge of communications

WAC: Women's Army Corps

GI: a member of the United Stated armed forces

Victory Gardens: home gardens planted with vegetables to increase food production during World War II

ration: a fixed share or allowance

Discussion Question Unemployment quickly disappeared as the United States went to war. FDR issued an executive order banning the common practice of closing skilled jobs to blacks, and Congress passed the Fair Employment Practices Act, which banned discrimination in government and defense industries. Women joined the work force to do jobs that had been held by men. Encourage students to discuss whether they think the war helped African-Americans and women in their struggle for equal rights in the years that followed.

Writing Prompt As the poet describes, Americans met the challenges of being at war with optimism, resourcefulness, and courage. Ask students to think about challenges they've faced. Then ask them to write a paragraph telling about a time when they remained optimistic or courageous in the face of a challenge.

Extension Activity Hand out copies of the poem on page 67. Then have students work in pairs to ask older Americans if the poem is consistent with their memories of World War II. What other memories do they have? Where were they when Pearl Harbor was attacked? Have students share the stories they obtained in class.

AMERICAN HISTORY POEMS
Scholastic Professional Books, 1998

Remembering Jim Crow

Rosa Parks: Montgomery, Alabama, December, 1955

I'd been working for years to change Jim Crow rules—
laws that kept our children in second rate schools.
And those buses! Thorns in my people's side
that prickled each time we paid for a ride.

> A dime doesn't care
> if you're white or you're black.
> Why should we pay full fare
> for a place in the back?

Then one evening on the first of December,
my name became a name people *still* remember.
Was that the first time Rosa Parks caused a fuss?
I'd been evicted *before* from a city bus.

> A dime doesn't care
> if you're white or you're black.
> Why should we pay full fare
> for a place in the back?

But that time the driver went for a cop
and started something Jim Crow couldn't stop.
When Montgomery police arrested ME,
they released the strength of a community.

> A dime doesn't care
> if you're white or you're black.
> Why should we pay full fare
> for a place in the back?

I just did what I *always* was ready to do.
It was the *driver* who started the hullabaloo.
Memories dim. Now his name is a mystery,
while I march on as a footnote in history.

Remembering Jim Crow
The Civil Rights Movement

On December 1, 1955, black woman named Rosa Parks was coming home from work. She sat down in the first row of seats *behind* the "White Only" section of the bus. When the "White section" filled, the driver told the people in Rosa Parks' row to stand. The others did. But, with conscious resolve, Parks stayed seated until she was arrested and taken to jail. The black community responded with a well-organized boycott of the bus company. About a year later, the Supreme Court declared that bus segregation was unconstitutional. By that time television had brought a most persuasive and inspiring young man into homes throughout America. He was a Baptist minister—Dr. Martin Luther King, Jr.

Under the leadership of Dr. King and a group of other dedicated leaders, the civil rights movement began to move forward with new momentum. The whole country—and then the world—watched the drama unfold. White supporters, especially students and religious leaders joined the growing ranks of blacks in the struggle.

In June of 1963, President John F. Kennedy asked Congress to pass a civil rights bill to end unfair treatment of blacks. The March on Washington was organized to support that bill. Over 250,000 people converged on Washington, D.C. The highlight of the day was Martin Luther King, Jr., as he described his dream of a world where all people would be treated equally.

VOCABULARY
Jim Crow: the segregation, or separation of African Americans

evicted: to be forced out of a place

Discussion Question Martin Luther King, Jr., was the youngest person to be awarded the Nobel Peace Prize. He believed that using peaceful means like passive resistance was better than fighting with weapons. Encourage the class to discuss whether they believe that nonviolent resistance actually works.

Writing Prompt Play a recording of Martin Luther King, Jr.'s, "I Have a Dream" speech. Allow the class to hear the rhythm of his words and visualize the pictures he paints. Have students write their own "dreams" for a better, more just, world.

Extension Activity Have students work in groups to research some other important events in the civil rights struggle. When they have finished, have them report their findings to the rest of the class.

AMERICAN HISTORY POEMS
Scholastic Professional Books, 1998

The Moon Dust Footprint

Joshua Katz: Croton-on-Hudson, New York, July 20, 1969

We'd been watching, watching, watching
all day long into the night—
    Mission Control in Houston,
       Apollo astronauts in flight.
A new chapter of history
    was about to open soon.
The Apollo slowed…then quickened,
speeding closer to the moon.

The others went to bed,
but not Aunt Mary and me.
We kept watching, watching, watching
    each slow step on the TV:
       the hovering Landing Module,
         the Sea of Tranquillity,
           and the astronaut, Neil Armstrong,
             moving oh so carefully…
I was holding my breath
    —Aunt Mary said she'd held hers, too—
until we saw the moon dust footprint
    made by Armstrong's ribbed left shoe!
That footprint marked a moment—
    an awesome human victory.
We were watching history happen—
    my Aunt Mary…and me.

The Moon Dust Footprint

"One Giant Leap for Mankind": The Moon Landing

In 1957 the Soviet Union dazzled the world by successfully launching Sputnik, the first satellite to circle Earth. Four years later, Soviet cosmonaut Yuri A. Gagarin became the first person to orbit Earth. Less than a year later, an American astronaut, John Glenn, Jr., matched Gagarin's feat. When Alan Shepard became the United States' "First Man in Space" in 1961, it seemed possible for humans to land on the moon and return safely to Earth. President John F. Kennedy was determined that the United States get to the moon first! Appealing to Congress for funding, he said, "No space project will be more exciting or more impressive to mankind...." And so the greatest adventure—and the greatest scientific and engineering challenge of human history—began in earnest. Over 350,000 people worked on the project.

On July 16, 1969, Apollo 11 cleared the launch tower at the Kennedy Space Center with three astronauts inside it. Four days later, two of them, Neil Armstrong and Edwin "Buzz" Aldrin, were walking and cavorting on the moon—239,000 miles from Earth! Meanwhile the third astronaut, Michael Collins, stayed in lunar orbit in the command module. Satellite television enabled millions of people all over the world to share the experience in less than two seconds after it happened.

VOCABULARY

Houston: city in Texas where the Johnson Space Center is located

landing module: part of a spacecraft designed for landing

Discussion Question One of the first things that the astronauts did was to place an American flag on the moon. The moon is windless, but the flag was wired to look as if it were blowing. The astronauts also left medals honoring five men who had died in the Soviet and American space programs, and an olive branch, the traditional symbol of peace. Ask students to discuss what they think the United States wanted to show by these symbolic gestures.

Writing Prompt For centuries the moon has tickled the human imagination, inspiring myths and stories. Ask students to try writing poems about the moon that reflect either their own personal images or those they imagine earlier Americans might have had. (Emphasize that the poems need not rhyme.) Have students share the poems with each other some Monday—or "Moon Day."

Extension Activity The space program enables scientists to learn a vast amount about the universe. Americans now work with other countries on various space projects. Have students work in teams to research current achievements of our space program.